Arran, Joney
and the
Ice Elves

A tale from the Wyrm Saga

Richard Middleton

First edition

12345678910

Copyright © 2017 Richard Middleton

All rights reserved.

ISBN: 1546827471
ISBN-13: 978-1546827474

FOR EVE AND RUBY

1

The air was bitterly cold, and rich with all the enticing smells of the Yule Fair.

'Roast chestnuts,' said Joney, breathing in with huge satisfaction, 'and caramel hazelnuts.'

Arran filled his lungs with scented air. 'Hot spiced cider,' he announced. 'Roast goose.'

'Cinnamon rolls.'

'Hog roast.'

'Mincemeat pies.'

'Mulled punch.'

'Venison stew!'

They grinned delightedly at each other.

It had been cold for weeks, really cold, and the High Canal had frozen over. The Wormwell townsfolk had taken full advantage and this year's Yule Fair had taken to the ice with a vengeance. Iron-edged skates had been dusted off and oiled and the leather made supple with grease. Toboggans and sleds of every kind and age had been pressed into service.

A village of tented stalls had grown up on the ice, offering every kind of festive food, drink and entertainment, at night lit by oil lanterns and warmed by the flames from wrought iron braziers raised high above the frozen surface.

The Yule Fair brought together rich and poor, the highest in society and the lowest. Arran and Joney were the lowest, there was no doubt about that. Runaways scratching a living on the stoneways and canals, they (and many others like them) were called water-rats. Or, more usually, 'hey, you little thieves, bring that back right now!'

They wandered agog through the fair, eyes stretched ever wider at the vast array of finely-wrought goods on offer, their senses wrapped in the warming glow of uncountable twinkling lights and the mingled scents of woodsmoke and hot food.

'A Hog Roast Special with hot cider, followed by mincemeat pies,' said Joney dreamily. 'Or should I go for Venison Stew, eggnog and a cinnamon roll?'

Arran let him dream. They had no more than a couple of iron pennies between them and he hadn't seen anything yet at the fair that they could afford.

But Arran had faith that something would turn up. And if it didn't, he'd have to make it.

Ahead of them a group of well-dressed boys and a girl in a beautiful fur-trimmed winter coat warmed themselves around the big fire at the end of the main avenue. They drank from steaming mugs. The boys laughed uproariously at something the finest dressed boy said. The girl smiled.

Arran and Joney sidled round the other side of the fire to warm their frozen hands and faces. The fire-keeper, a stout old woman with a face like a wrinkled red apple, narrowed her eyes when she saw them.

She was posted there to stop thieves and pickpockets from preying on the crowds of shoppers and skaters drawn to the fire. Arran and Joney sat squarely in the thieves and pickpockets category and, with their shabby clothes and unkempt looks, were clearly undesirable.

Still, thought Arran, it's Yule. Maybe…

Arran nervously caught the old woman's

eye. After a moment's pause and a hard stare she nodded. Arran nodded his thanks back.

He held his hands to the fire and felt the tingle in his chilled fingers as they began to thaw.

As the flames leapt and danced, Arran caught scattered glimpses through them of the girl and her companions.

Arran, fifteen years old and short on friends except for twelve-year old Joney, was lonely. The girl was about his age and to Arran's eyes as pretty as a winged, spun-glass Valkyrie he'd seen on a stall earlier. She had long gold-coloured hair and a mischievous expression.

She caught his eye and winked. Arran felt himself blush.

'Hey! Keep your eyes to yourself, water-rat scum! That's my girlfriend.'

Arran jumped guiltily. He hadn't seen the biggest boy from the group make his way around the side of the fire towards him. The boy was a couple of years older than Arran. His face was flushed and his eyes glassy.

'You, old woman! What'd you think you're doing letting these water-rats in with the rest of us decent folk?'

The boy pointed an unsteady hand at the fire-keeper.

'Are you too old and feeble to do your job properly?'

The old woman squinted at him.

'I'm Cydric Sloe,' announced the boy. 'My father runs this fair,' he said loudly, 'which means I do too. And I think you've just decided to look for a new job.'

'It's Yule,' said Arran quietly. 'She was just being kind.'

Cydric stepped towards him. Arran could smell the sickly fumes of mead on his breath. Cydric jabbed his finger at Arran's chest.

'I'm going to call the wardens and have you thrown out of here! It's thieving scum like you who ruin Yule for everyone!'

But before he could draw breath to shout for the wardens, something utterly miraculous appeared in the winter sky.

Everyone stopped, transfixed.

Sweeping down through the low grey clouds came a large wooden sleigh pulled by a team of pure white reindeer. Seated on the sleigh was an old, fat, jolly-looking man with white hair and a big white beard. He was dressed in a white coat and trousers edged with white fur.

Arran and Joney watched open-mouthed as the reindeer pulled the sleigh in a wide circle around the Yule Fair, flying effortlessly through the freezing air, higher than the highest building on the High Canal.

The man in white waved to the onlookers. Every child waved back. Some adults did too.

Arran could hear the ringing sound of the silver bells fastened to the harnesses and the sides of the sleigh.

Joney rubbed his eyes. 'Are you seeing what I'm seeing?'

'Maybe, but I'm not sure I believe it.'

'Who is that old man?'

As if to answer Joney, the old man shouted down in a booming, laughing voice: 'Merryman is near! Merryman brings good cheer! Merryman brings merriment to everyone here!'

The crowds erupted in cheers and applause. They were merry enough already, but the promise of even more merriment was to be celebrated wholeheartedly.

The sleigh circled once again, then slowly descended to the ice. It touched down in a flurry of ice crystals half a mile further down the High Canal, then slowly made its way up the frozen way towards the fair. Outlying skaters, entranced by the spectacle, accompanied the sleigh so by the time it reached the main avenue a crowd had gathered around it.

'Gather round, good people, gather round,' said Merryman, his voice carrying far through the crisp air.

The crowd grew larger as more people left what they were doing to join the throng around the sleigh.

'I have gifts for everyone!' announced Merryman.

The crowd's cheers were deafening.

'I need a good-hearted child to be the bearer of my gifts,' boomed Merryman. He jumped out of the sleigh with surprising agility and stepped into the crowd.

The crowd parted to let him through.

Arran and Joney, who had only caught glimpses of Merryman through the eager throng, were surprised to find the crowds parting around them as Merryman came towards the fire.

'Is he coming towards us?' Joney whispered nervously.

'No way,' said Arran reassuringly. 'We're thieving water-rats, remember? No-one could ever accuse us of being good-hearted.'

Secretly Arran felt that perhaps someone as magical as Merryman should know that he and Joney were only thieves through necessity, and that deep down they were as good hearted as anyone else.

Arran hoped that Merryman would choose Joney. The poor kid hadn't had much of a start in life or much luck in his twelve years of existence. Being chosen as a gift-bearer, and proclaimed to all and wide as a good-hearted child, was the kind of event in a boy's life that could turn things around for him for good.

Merryman stopped and made a show of warming his hands on the fire.

But he's not close enough to the fire to feel the warmth, thought Arran suddenly. But no-one else seemed to have noticed.

Merryman put his hands on his hips and chortled 'Ho! Ho! Ho!'

The crowd chuckled along.

Merryman turned to look at Arran and Joney.

The crowd took in a collective breath. Was one of these children to be the gift-bearer?

Arran looked at Joney, willing Merryman to choose his friend.

But there was silence. When Arran glanced back at Merryman, the old man was frowning at them deeply, as if what he saw displeased him greatly.

The boys shrank back, feeling the mood of the crowd turn against them.

Fortunately Merryman turned away from them to Cydric's group.

Merryman raised a fat old hand and pointed directly at Cydric.

Cydric grinned smugly.

'What's your name, child?' boomed Merryman.

'Cydric Sloe!' shouted Cydric.

'You, good child Cydric, will be the bearer of my wondrous gifts!'

The crowd cheered.

3.

'This is all wrong,' muttered Arran. He grabbed Joney's arm and pulled him into the crowd away from Merryman and Cydric.

'I thought it was going to be me,' said Joney miserably.

'I think you're lucky it wasn't,' said Arran.

Joney looked at him, startled.

'What d'you mean?'

'There's no way that Cydric boy is good-hearted,' said Arran. 'And did you see how Merryman only pretended to warm his hands on the fire?'

Joney shook his head.

'I don't think he's what he appears,' said Arran. 'I think there's something else going on. I wouldn't want to be in Cydric's shoes right now.'

Joney cheered up. 'So I might be good-hearted after all?'

Arran stopped and stared at his friend. 'Joney, of course you're good-hearted! You might be a bit thick sometimes, and take being irritating to extraordinary heights, but there's absolutely no doubt at all that you're one of the goodest-hearted people I've ever known.'

Joney beamed with pride. 'Thanks Arran!'

They pushed their way through the last of the crowd and out onto the almost-empty main avenue.

'Even the stallholders have gone to watch,' said Arran. That was worrying too. Stallholders needed trade, they needed to feed their families. Abandoning their stalls was against their very nature.

He noticed Joney has strayed near to an unmanned baker's stall. 'Hey, what have you got there?'

Joney hid something behind his back and shrugged. 'Nothing.'

Arran was about to say more when a movement on the stall caught his eye.

'Did you see that?'

'What?'

Something glittering in the air, like a wisp of ice crystals blown in the wind. Then it was gone, as if it had never been.

'I'm not sure.'

Arran stepped forward to examine the stall more closely. 'Show me what you took from here,' he told Joney.

Joney reluctantly brought his hand from behind his back and showed Arran two mincemeat pies.

'They're hot?'

'Of course.'

'Well, these aren't.' Arran pointed to the mincemeat pies on the stall. 'They're frozen solid.'

'They can't be.'

Joney stepped forward to see. The glitter of frost lay over everything. The pies, pastries and sausage rolls were as cold and hard as ice. The brazier at the back of the stall was as black and dead as if it had been extinguished days ago.

Arran shivered.

'Come on,' he said. 'Let's get out of here. I don't like this at all.'

Arran led Joney quickly through the maze of tented stalls, away from the main avenue and the frost-touched baker's stall.

But as they went, Arran glimpsed more of the glittering wisps of ice crystals, drifting down the icy paths, slipping into the tented stalls, leaving a hard frost over everything they touched.

'I saw something,' whispered Joney.

'They're everywhere,' said Arran grimly.

'What are they?

What had Arran actually seen? Mostly a shimmer of frosted air, easily dismissed as the play of wind on loose ice. But now his eye was attuned to seeing the creatures, he thought he saw a shape loosely binding the glitter together.

A small, slender, human-shaped form, no bigger than a crow or raven.

'Some kind of elf, perhaps,' he guessed. His mother had reads him tales of elves, witches and goblins when he was young. She'd read about them as if they were real.

That was before she'd died and things had started to go bad in Arran's life.

'Not the good kind of elf,' Joney shivered. 'Not if they're freezing everything.'

'Ice elves, then. Maybe they came down from the North.'

'With Merryman?'

Arran thought about that. He nodded slowly. 'That's right. All the more reason for getting away from here.'

They were nearing the edge of the Yule Fair village.

'Wait,' said Joney. 'We have to eat these before they get cold.'

He held up the two mincemeat pies.

Arran nodded. If ice elves were freezing everything in the Yule Fair, there was no point in wasting the last of the hot food.

Joney handed him one and took a luxurious bite out of the other.

'That is sooooo delicious,' mumbled Joney through a warm mouthful of pastry and filling.

Arran raised his own mincemeat pie to his mouth. He smelled the rich, warm, spicy scents of the mincemeat filling. His mouth started to water.

He was about to take a deep, satisfying bite into the sweet pastry when he saw a swirl of movement ahead, a frosty glittering in the air around a dark shape huddled against the side of the stall ahead.

'Hey!' he shouted. The ice elves seemed to be clustered around the motionless figure.

The ice elves scattered as they approached.

It was an old man. He was wrapped in a ragged cloak that might once have been red with white fur trimmings, but was now faded and browned. He looked as if he had walked for many, many miles and finally reached the end of the road.

He has wispy white hair and a long, tangled white beard. His face was wrinkled and weather-beaten. His skin sparkled with a dusting of frost.

He didn't move as they approached
'Is he dead?' whispered Joney.

4.

Arran leaned closer to the old man, listening for breathing.

He heard nothing. Not a sound from the old man. Not a movement.

'He's dead, isn't he?' whispered Joney. 'Poor old bogger. I'd have given him my mincemeat pie if he'd been alive.'

At his words a tremor ran through the old man's body like spring through winter ice.

The boys jumped back in surprise.

The old man's frostbitten lips opened and he took in a long shuddering breath.

He whispered something faintly.

Arran leaned closer to hear.

'Pie,' repeated the old man.

Arran sighed. He'd hoped for something more profound.

'At least he has his priorities right,' said Joney.

Arran pressed his warm mincemeat pie to the old man's lips. The pie was gone in a flash.

'Blimey,' said Joney, impressed. 'He's

hungrier even than me.'

He gingerly lowered his half-eaten pie to the old man's mouth and that, too was instantly consumed.

The old man's breathing became more regular and some of his colour returned.

The old man shifted uncomfortably. Then he started to make a horrible creaking noise.

Arran thought he was dying.

'Is he singing?' asked Joney.

Arran strained to hear. The old man was indeed singing, although very badly.

'I think it's that carol,' said Joney. He had sharper hearing than Arran. '*Gods rest ye merry gentlemen.*'

Arran listened carefully, then nodded. He recognised the chorus.

The old man continued his carol, moving his lips painfully.

'We have to go,' said Arran. What else could they do to help the old man?

The beggar reached out a desperate hand to clutch at Arran's sleeve.

'Listen,' he rasped. Then he sang the verse again, very badly.

Arran listened. Then he realised that old man was singing different words in the verse than he'd ever heard before.

'The night the old sun dies,
And cold seeks to prevail,
Frey's tear will reveal the lie,
And merry men will fail.
And good tidings of comfort and joy...'

Joney shuddered. 'That doesn't sound good at all. *And merry men will fail.*'

'It's tonight,' said Arran in surprise. 'Tonight's the night the old sun dies. Midwinter night.'

He stared at the old man, trying to make sense of what he was seeing and hearing.

Why was the old man singing those words when he'd been so near death just a few moments before?

They must be important to him. But why?

Arran turned the words over in his mind, looking for the answer.

He thought back to the frost-covered goods on the stalls and the glitter of ice crystals drifting purposefully through the fair.

'It must all be happening tonight,' he said. 'Not just the death of the old sun. The rest of it too. It's the ice elves. They must be *the cold* that *seeks to prevail.*'

The old man twitched and muttered something.

'What?' Arran bent closer to hear.

'Iselven?'

'Ice elves, yes,' said Arran. 'They're

everywhere.'

'Here,' muttered the old man. 'Take.'

He reached out a scarred, gnarled hand that looked as old as tree roots, and dropped a few small, red objects into their outstretched palms.

Holly berries.

'Thanks,' said Joney dubiously.

'Protect you,' grunted the old man. 'Against the iselfen. But not the king. For him you need…' He gasped suddenly and went silent. He pawed pathetically at his mouth.

Arran was horrified to see that the inside of the old beggar's mouth had frosted over.

After a few moments the old man's pain seemed to ease

'What do the ice elves want?'

The old man was silent for a moment, then he raised a bony finger to his lips and whispered, 'Listen.'

The boys listened, and heard nothing. Silence reigned throughout the Yule Fair.

'What?' said Joney. 'I can't hear anything.'

Then Arran understood.

The sounds of the Yule fair should have filled their ears. Laughter, singing, excitement, and a tumult of light and fire that held back the ice and cold. On the night of the death of the old sun, these joyful, bright, warming things summoned the new sun to bring life to the New Year.

'The ice elves want the ice to stay,' said

Arran suddenly. 'They love the cold. They want a cold sun to be born, not a warm sun.'

The old man nodded slowly. 'Yes. They want a colder world.'

Joney shivered. 'It's cold enough already.'

'What can we do?' asked Arran hopelessly. What could they do against such dreadful things?

In response the old beggar simply sighed and began to sing his carol once more.

'Great,' said Joney. 'I needed to hear that again.'

Arran heard a noise behind him.

He looked up.

A middle-aged man was shuffling towards him. Arran recognised him as one of the stallholders. His clothes, skin and hair glittered with white frost. He held a gaily decorated present tightly in his hands. His face was expressionless.

'Back off!' shouted Arran hopefully.

The man showed no sign of hearing. He kept on coming.

'More snowmen coming from the other side,' muttered Joney.

Arran noticed that every single one of them held a gift tightly in their hands.

'It's the presents,' exclaimed Joney, noticing the same thing. 'Don't let them touch you! Cydric was handing them out to people, remember? And look what happened to them.'

Arran noticed a glittering in the air behind the shuffling, frosted townsfolk.

'Ice elves!' he whispered to Joney. 'They're driving the snowmen towards us!'

'I had noticed.'

'Why don't they just attack us themselves? Freeze us like they did the pies?'

'Does it matter?' asked Joney gloomily. 'Because now we're surrounded.'

5

In response Arran leapt forward and threw himself headfirst at the feet of the nearest snowman. He slid on the ice and smashed hard into the frost-covered shins.

The snowman pitched up into the air.

Arran kept on sliding. He held his handful of holly berries above his head and the ice elves fled from them, shrieking with high-pitched voices like wind through frost-stiff leaves.

The snowman crashed to the ice behind him and lay motionless.

'Come on, then,' Arran shouted to Joney, who had watched events with an open mouth. 'Let's go!'

Joney started to run, then kicked into a slide. He jumped over the fallen snowman, landed tidily and continued the slide all the way up to Arran.

'Neat,' said Arran appreciatively.

Joney grinned.

Goaded by the ice elves, the remaining

snowmen turned and started shuffling towards them.

The boys turned and ran.

They twisted and turned through the maze of stalls and booths and soon left the snowmen behind. They saw more, though, as they ran through the frozen alleyways and backstreets, and had to keep doubling back and taking different routes to avoid them.

Arran was sad to see that some of the frost-gripped townspeople had frozen up entirely, like icy statues staring down at their fatal gifts.

'What do we do now?' panted Joney. 'That old man's carol was just doom and gloom. It didn't help at all.'

Arran had been wondering about that. The old beggar had helped them by giving them the holly berries to protect them against the ice elves. So he wanted them stop the ice elves.

'Maybe the rest of the verse wasn't a warning,' he said. 'Maybe it was an answer.'

'How?' said Joney sceptically. 'And why would we want merry men to fail?'

Arran thought about that. Then he grinned.

'We would if there was just one of them.'

Joney looked puzzled.

Then he got it. 'One merry man!' he said delightedly. 'Merryman!'

'Exactly.'

Then Arran sobered. 'But I have no idea what Frey's tear is.'

'Me neither.'

They were so caught up the puzzle that they round around a corner and almost ran straight into a snowman on the other side.

Arran was about charge in and knock it down when he realised it wasn't a snowman at all.

It was the girl who had winked at him earlier.

The girl with the long gold-coloured hair and the smile.

Except she wasn't smiling. She looked angry and upset.

She stopped when she saw them and looked more cheerful.

'Oh, hello again.'

'What happened?'

'Oh, stupid Cydric. He was handing out presents for everyone but he forgot me. So I left.'

'Was he acting strange?'

The girl frowned and thought back. 'Maybe he was. Difficult to tell with Cydric. Sometimes he's fun as summer, sometimes he's cold as ice. He did have too much to drink earlier, which made him behave stupidly, but then after Merryman chose Cydric to give the gifts out he just ignored me.'

She looked upset again.

Arran thought about what she said, and about the icebound people they'd seen wandering through the fair.

'Maybe not,' he said slowly. He really didn't like Cydric, but he didn't like being unfair to people either. 'Or, rather, perhaps he ignored you to protect you. We've seen what happens to people who receive one of Merryman's gifts.'

'They freeze up,' said Joney.

'They what?' the girl looked puzzled.

'Freeze up. They take their present and go off to open it. But before they can they just freeze solid. Or they become a snowman.'

The girl shivered.

'I don't like the sound of that.' Then she brightened. 'So maybe Cydric actually cares for me after all.'

Arran shrugged. 'Possibly.' That was as far as he was prepared to go in defending the obnoxious Cydric.

A sudden glittering in the air behind her made him anxious.

He stepped forward.

'This may seem a bit strange,' he said, 'but please take this. It'll protect you. Merryman's gifts aren't the only danger out here tonight.'

He held out one of the holly berries that the old beggar had given her.

She smiled suddenly. 'Shouldn't that be mistletoe?'

Arran blushed.

She grinned at him mischievously. 'Freya

would approve.'

Arran stared at her.

'What did you say?'

'That's who mistletoe comes from, silly.' She laughed. 'The goddess of love. Didn't you know? Mistletoe berries are the tears that Freya wept when the trickster Loki slew Baldur.'

'That's it!' said Arran, astonished, remembering the strange verse in the carol the old beggar had sung. 'Mistletoe! That's the answer!'

He'd realised how they could defeat Merryman.

He was so caught up with excitement that he forgot himself and impulsively kissed the laughing face before him.

The girl kissed him back enthusiastically.

After a few moments (the longest in Arran's life) Joney coughed politely.

The two parted. Despite the bitterly cold night Arran felt as warm as if he'd been standing before a fire all day.

The girl grinned at him. 'Happy Yuletide,' she said.

'Merryman,' whispered Joney.

Arran nodded. 'We have to go. I'm Arran.'

'Nice kissing you, Arran', said the girl, smiling. 'I'm Gretta.

'Keep hold of that holly berry,' said Arran seriously. 'It's important.'

'Of course,' said Gretta. 'It's my present

from you. And here's mine to you.'

She stepped forward and kissed him again.

Again time seemed to stop for Arran.

Eventually Joney had to cough very loudly.

'Got to go,' mumbled Arran, extricating himself unwillingly.

'Bye Arran.' Gretta smiled farewell.

'Bye Gretta.'

'Come on,' said Joney impatiently.

But Arran watched Gretta make her way out of the Yule Fair and head home before he and Joney started back towards the crowd and Merryman.

6.

'Mistletoe!' said Arran. 'Mistletoe berries are Frey's tears!'

'I saw some mistletoe,' said Joney excitedly.

'Where?'

'On a stall. Somewhere near the venison stew seller.'

'Let's go get it.'

But around the next corner they slid to a halt. The way was blocked by a crowd of frost-gripped townspeople.

Arran and Joney backtracked and tried another route, but again the way was blocked.

'If you draw them off, I'll get the mistletoe,' said Joney.

It was the sensible choice, except for one thing. Joney wasn't very reliable.

Time and again Arran had trusted him to complete a task alone, and time and again Joney had failed. He was too young, too easily distracted.

Arran shook his head. 'We have to go together,' he said.

But he knew that wouldn't work. There were too many of the frost-gripped snowmen.

Joney looked at his friend desperately. 'I can do it, Arran. I promise.'

The crowds of snowmen were drawing in from all sides.

Arran was in an agony of indecision. He had to trust Joney, but he knew he couldn't.

'I don't even know what we'll do when we get the mistletoe,' said Arran.

'Oh, I do,' said Joney. 'I have a plan.'

'You have a plan?' said Arran in disbelief.

'That's right.'

Arran studied his friend carefully.

Joney looked back at him with wide eyes.

'Go,' said Arran, finally. 'I'll draw them off as long as I can. It's up to you now.'

Joney nodded. 'Thanks.'

Then Joney slipped under the canvas side of the tented stall behind them and was gone.

The nearest snowman was just feet away. Arran dodged him and started to run.

The next few minutes were the most exhausting of his life. He ran, ducked, dodged, slid and scrambled his way through the icy fair, hounded by scores of frost-gripped townspeople.

Every moment he evaded them was a moment longer for Joney to find the mistletoe and carry out the plan.

But he began to tire. He'd not eaten

anything all day and his body was cold and weary.

There seemed to be fewer and fewer open pathways to escape down, and eventually Arran realised that he was being herded in a particular direction.

Then there was just one route left, and he half ran, half slid down it until he saw who was waiting at the end of it.

Merryman.

There was nowhere else to go.

Arran walked down the icy path towards him. The fat old man's booming laughter rang in his ears.

When he was a few feet away, Arran prepared to throw the precious contents of his clenched fist at Merryman.

For a moment a faint shadow of worry crossed Merryman's face.

Arran completed his throw.

His handful of red holly berries bounced off Merryman's fat stomach and rolled away into the crowd.

'Ho! Ho! Ho!' chortled Merryman. 'That doesn't work on me, young man.'

He grinned at Arran. 'Now it's time for me to give you a gift.'

7.

'Cydric Sloe,' boomed Merryman. 'Bring this boy a gift. Bring him the biggest, brightest, best gift on my sleigh!'

Cydric shuffled slowly towards the sleigh, his icy clothes cracking as he moved.

Arran watched him.

'Don't you want my gift,' boy? Merryman loomed over Arran. 'Everyone loves my gifts.'

Arran looked around at the cold, mean faces of the townspeople crowding around the sleigh, as they waited for their present.

Cydric pushed his way through the silent throng and lifted a large, brightly-wrapped present from the sack at the back of the sleigh.

He trudged back with the gift, his face blank and frosted with ice crystals.

'My gift to you,' said Merryman. He leaned in towards Arran, as if sharing a secret.

'Shall I tell you what's in it? Because you'll never find out.'

Arran stared into Merryman's eyes and his heart seemed to shrink inside him. The thing that looked out of Merryman's eyes was cold in a way that Arran had never imagined.

'It's a cold heart,' whispered Merryman. 'Just for you.'

The thing inside Merryman loved ice, and stillness, and the ending of life.

Cydric came towards Arran with the gift.

Arran prayed to all the gods that Joney really did have a plan, and that it would work.

Cydric started to hand the gift to Arran. Arran leaned back desperately, trying to stop the brightly decorated wrapping paper from touching him.

Where was Joney?

'Happy Yuletide!' Merryman leaned back and guffawed, hands on his hips, mouth wide open with fake merriment.

'Ho, Ho...' he chortled.

There was a twang in the distance and a snow- white berry zipped through the air.

It flew straight into Merryman's mouth, right in mid-'*Ho*'.

Merryman looked surprised and swallowed involuntarily.

His face distorted with sudden fear.

"And a Happy Yuletide to you too!" screamed out Joney in the distance. He waved his favourite catapult in triumph.

Merryman screamed.

Cydric turned to look at the old man. The present dropped, forgotten, from his fingers onto the ice.

Arran breathed again.

Merryman howled with frustration and anger. Cracks appeared across his skin like cracks in thin ice.

'Frey's tear will reveal the lie, and *Merryman* will fail,' shouted Arran.

Merryman shook as if caught in a maelstrom. The cracks in his skin widened and blinding ice-blue light glared out from within.

Merryman wailed.

Then he shattered.

The blue light burst through the icy shell, scattering pieces across the confused crowd.

The king of the iselfen was revealed inside, his disguise destroyed. As tall as a man, he seemed barely more than a storm of ice crystals whirling within a roughly human shape.

The mistletoe berry burned brightly in his chest.

The iselfen king clawed at it, trying fruitlessly to remove it. But the more frantic he got, the stronger the mistletoe light glowed, until the iselfen king let out an unearthly, high pitched screech and began to spin around in a blaze of white-blue light, faster and faster.

He spun so fast that he became just a blur of light. Then he shot up into the air like a firework, trailing a comet-tail of sparks.

He flew far up into the frozen night sky above Wormwell. So high that Arran could see nothing more of him than a shimmering point of light, hanging there for a moment like a new star.

Then with a sound like a million ice crystals smashing, and a final despairing cry, the king of the iselfen burst into a blizzard of glowing white snowflakes.

8.

The crowd sighed, as if released from a spell.

The glowing snowflakes drifted down over the Yule Fair.

Arran got to his feet just in time to be knocked over again by Joney who ran into him, full of excitement.

'I did it, Arran! I did it.'

Arran dusted himself off and hugged his friend.

'You did too, Joney. Well done. That was a truly mighty shot.'

Joney sobered for a moment. 'I was so worried, and my hands were shaking. But then it was like there were people helping me, steadying me, and I took the shot.'

Arran remember his prayer to the gods, and smiled to himself.

'Gentlemen,' said a kind voice behind them.

They turned to see the old beggar who had given them the holly berries and sung them the carol *Gods Rest Ye Merry Gentlemen*.

'You have my joyful thanks,' said the old man.

He looked better than when they'd seen him last. His white hair was curlier, and his long beard shone. His clothes seemed brighter and newer.

'The iselfen king captured me and stole my face, my form and my magic,' said the old man. 'And he set the iselfen to harry me wherever I went. All I could do was to follow him and hope that one day someone would listen to my carol, and understand.'

He smiled merrily at Arran and Joney. 'Which you did.'

He bowed to them.

'What about everyone who was given a gift?' said Arran. 'He froze them!'

'Watch,' smiled the old man.

The glowing snowflakes drifted down from the bitter sky and wherever they landed on one of the affected townspeople, it melted the ice magic and filled them with warmth and hope.

All around them, people were shaking themselves and, suddenly, smiling. Friendly chatter started up, and children's joyful cries rang out again as they saw the delights of the fair.

Arran watched as a snowflake fell lightly onto Cydric's nose. After a moment, Cydric shuddered and a smile lit up his face.

He looked around frantically. 'Where's…?'

'Gretta went home,' said Arran.

'Oh,' said Cydric. 'I should go, then. I have to speak to her.'

Arran nodded.

Cydric looked worried. 'I'm sorry,' he said. 'I was a total snit earlier. Don't know what came over me.' He dug into his pockets and pulled out a couple of tokens. 'Take these,' he said, 'they'll give you the run of the fair.'

'Thanks!' said Joney.

They watched Cydric go.

'I noticed that you didn't tell Cydric that you kissed his girlfriend,' said Joney, grinning. 'Twice.'

Arran blushed. 'I suspect that Yuletide good-fellowship only goes so far,' he said.

He turned to the old man who'd looked like a beggar but who now looked more and more like Merryman, but with red clothes rather than white.

'You're Merryman, then? I mean, the real one?'

Merryman laughed. 'Exactly so, my boy. Klaus Merryman at your service. Now returning to his full glory.'

He walked over to the sleigh. The reindeer snuffled happily into his outstretched hands.

'Hello, old friends,' said Merryman. 'I missed you very much.'

He walked to the back of the sleigh and peered at the wrapped boxes in the back.

'Are they still dangerous?' Arran regarded them anxiously.

'Empty boxes, now,' said Merryman. 'But some danger still remains, if folks count a gift above the person that gave it.'

He gathered the sack and with a mighty effort flung it high into the sky, where it disappeared in a shimmer of multi-coloured lights and a faint ringing of bells.

'What will you do now?' asked Arran.

'Have a long rest!' laughed Merryman. 'But I'll be back every Yuletide.'

'Not with gifts,' said Arran. He shuddered, remembering Cydric advancing towards him with a cold heart wrapped in a brightly decorated box.

'Not with gifts,' agreed Merryman. 'I will come to remind people to have warm hearts,' he said. 'Nothing more than that. But there is no greater gift.'

Arran nodded.

'Happy Yuletide,' he said to Merryman.

'And to you,' replied the jolly old man.

'Happy Yuletide!' said Joney.

'And to you, merry gentleman.'

Klaus Merryman leapt onto his sleigh and laughed.

He shook the reins and the reindeer tossed their heads and antlers in response. Then the reindeer stepped forward, pulling the sleigh around, and started to pick up speed.

Arran and Joney watched the sleigh rush down the icy High Canal, then lift into the air. The sleigh gained height and then circled back over the fair.

They saw old man look down on them and wave joyfully.

'And merriment to you all!' His voice carried like clear bells across the Yule Fair, sparking excitement and joy and hope in all that heard it.

Then the sleigh rushed up into the clouds and was gone.

9.

Joney sighed. 'I'm still hungry,' he said.

There was a sudden shout from behind them.

'Hey, lads!'

They turned to see the roast goose seller waving his carving knife at them and smiling.

'Come here, lads. You look right hungry. How'd you fancy a nice pile of roast goose in a king-size bap?'

Joney stepped towards him, his face wistful.

'With gravy?'

The roast goose seller nodded. 'And sage and onion stuffing. Best there is!'

Joney swallowed hard.

Arran cut in before Joney could wind himself up any further.

'Thanks sir, but we don't have any money, sir. Thanks all the same.'

He took Joney's arm to lead him away.

'Wait. It's Yuletide, lads.'

The roast goose seller piled steaming meat into a fresh bap the size of a dinner plate. 'I wouldn't take your money even if you had some. This one's on me!'

Arran's heart skipped a beat. He looked around at the happy crowd and felt a sudden wave of warmth flood through him, like a long hug.

All around him the crowds of people were smiling, laughing, having fun, enjoying the Yuletide fair together.

Before, he hadn't felt a part of that crowd. He was a water-rat, an undesirable. But now he felt part of the festivities. Now he and Joney were part of it.

No, he realised, they weren't just *part* of it. They were at the centre of it. Together they had defeated the king of iselfen, and now, wonderfully, they had become the heart of the festive gathering.

Grinning, he pulled Joney forward towards the roast goose stall. 'Come on, Joney. What are you waiting for? Aren't you hungry?'

The delicious smell of roast meat, spicy stuffing and rich gravy filled their noses and made them dizzy.

'Merry Yuletide, lads!' The smiling stallholder handed them each a plate of steaming food. 'Enjoy!'

The boys grinned and mumbled their thanks through mouthfuls of hot, dripping goose.

They wandered through the fair, munching away, dazzled by the dozens of candles that lit every stall, the soft light shining off the glittering foil of the decorations and making the frosty ice underfoot sparkle.

'Hey, boys!' A woman at a stall selling hot drinks waved to them. 'How about a mug of hot spiced punch to go with that? On the house, of course.'

Another voice, across the way. 'And some Yule pudding, and a couple of mincemeat pies to go with it?'

Arran saw the candlelight sparkle in Joney's wondering eyes, and grinned a grin big enough to light up the entire Yule fair all on its own.

.....

Much, much later the boys staggered back to their hideout, stuffed and content.

'Happy Yuletide,' mumbled Joney sleepily from his bed in the other room. 'Remember those delicious mincemeat pies, and that wonderful hot roast goose, and the marvellous venison stew…?'

He started to snore, and then he ate, and ate, and ate all night in his dreams. And he never got full and enjoyed every single bite as much as the first.

But as Arran drifted off to sleep all he could remember was how time had stopped when Gretta kissed him, and all he dreamed about that wonderful night was long, gold-coloured hair and a mischievous smile.

ABOUT THE WYRM SAGA

Arran, Joney and the Ice Elves is a tale from
the Wyrm Saga, a linked set of novels and tales
set in a the North Country where children like
Arran and Joney are beginning to realise that
they share their world with ice elves, monster
plants, witches, wyrms and other magical
people and creatures.

The first two novels in the Wyrm Saga are
The Wyrm Conspiracy and *Wyrm Gold*.
The third book in the Wyrm Saga, *Wyrm
Prophecy*, is in development.

www.ingramcontent.com/pod-product-compliance
Lightning Source LLC
Chambersburg PA
CBHW032132050726
47590CB00008B/3063